V

D0842449

Uri Shulevitz

THE TREASURE

SQUARE
FISH

Farrar Straus Giroux
New York

SQUARE
FISH
An Imprint of Macmillan

ISBN 978-0-374-47955-8
Library of Congress catalog card number: 78-12952

Originally published in the United States by Farrar Straus Giroux
First Square Fish Edition: June 2012
Square Fish logo designed by Filomena Tuosto
mackids.com

28 30 29

AR: 3.0 / LEXILE: 490L

To Gertrude Hopkins,
and to Peter Hopkins,
who taught me the techniques of the Old Masters

There once was a man and his name was Isaac.

He lived in such poverty that again and again he went to bed hungry.

One night, he had a dream.

In his dream, a voice told him to go to the capital
city and look for a treasure under the bridge by the
Royal Palace.

"It is only a dream," he thought when he woke up,
and he paid no attention to it.

The dream came back a second time.
And Isaac still paid no attention to it.

When the dream came back a third time, he said,
"Maybe it's true," and so he set out on his journey.

Now and then, someone gave him a ride, but
most of the way he walked.

He walked through forests.

He crossed over mountains.

Finally he reached the capital city.

But when he came to the bridge by the Royal Palace, he found that it was guarded day and night.

He did not dare to search for the treasure.
Yet he returned to the bridge every morning and
wandered around it until dark.

One day, the captain of the guards asked him,
"Why are you here?"

Isaac told him the dream. The captain laughed.

"You poor fellow," he said, "what a pity you wore your shoes out for a dream! Listen, if I believed a dream I once had, I would go right now to the city you came from, and I'd look for a treasure under the stove in the house of a fellow named Isaac." And he laughed again.

Isaac bowed to the captain and started on his long
way home.

He crossed over mountains.

He walked through forests.

Now and then, someone gave him a ride, but most
of the way he walked.

At last, he reached his own town.

When he got home, he dug under his stove, and there he found the treasure.

In thanksgiving, he built a house of prayer, and in one of its corners he put an inscription: *Sometimes one must travel far to discover what is near.*

Isaac sent the captain of the guards a priceless ruby.
And for the rest of his days he lived in contentment
and he never was poor again.